Table of Contents

Chapter 1 – Valentine Notes

"Roses are red. Violets are blue. And these new donuts of yours sound too good to be true," Amy recited.

Heather laughed. "Your compliments sound even better when they're rhyming."

Her best friend shrugged. "I thought it was appropriate for Valentine's Day approaching."

"Don't remind me," Heather said. "I've got a million orders to fill for couples in love. And all my assistants are starry-eyed right now too. They're more focused on romance than baking."

As if they knew that they were being talked about, Nina and Janae walked into the kitchen of Donut Delights then. However, they were also behaving in ways to prove Heather's point. Janae was humming a romantic tune and practically dancing as she entered the room. Nina was smiling and blushing as she read a Valentine note.

"Good news?" Amy asked Nina.

The young assistant's face turned even redder than the card, and she pushed the note into her pocket. "It's just something sweet

from Nick. Since he works across the street, he's able to pop over and hand me Valentine clues. As long as his mean uncle, Mr. Rankle, isn't looking."

"Clues?" asked Heather curiously.

"Oh, not like for the types of cases that you investigate," Nina said quickly. "But Nick is planning a surprise for our Valentine's Day date. He's giving me hints about what we're doing in love note form."

"That sounds adorable," said Janae.

"It's a very caring and creative gesture," said Heather. "What sort of clues did he give you?"

Nina considered it for a moment and then decided to share. She took the Valentine out of her pocket and showed her friends. It was cut into the shape of a red heart and written on it was: We make quite a PAIR! And be sure to wear a pair of comfy shoes.

"That is very sweet," said Heather. "And it sounds like you'll be doing something besides just a romantic dinner."

"Maybe you're doing something similar to what Fire Frank and I are doing," said Janae. "We've been doing chocolate bike tours."

"I don't know how to feel about this," Amy joked as she put on a thoughtful face. "I love the first part of that idea. I'm not sure about the second."

"What is a chocolate bike tour?" asked Nina.

"It's something we've been experimenting with all this week. We ride our bikes past scenic and romantic spots on the island and then make our way to different places that have delicious chocolate. They're like candy pitstops along our way," Janae explained. "It's just for fun right now. But I might try and do it as a special event next year with the bike tours I lead for my second job. That is if we can figure out the perfect trail."

"I can see how finding that perfect trail could take a while," Amy teased, "if testing out all the different possibilities allows you two to spend time together as a couple and try lots of chocolate."

"Maybe we are taking our sweet time perfecting it," Janae admitted with a laugh.

"Well, if you do add a chocolate tour to your bike tours, please consider adding Donut Delights to it," said Heather. "I think we have some delicious chocolate options we could contribute."

"I'd love to," Janae said. "And if this ever does become a real event, I promise we will. Fire Frank and I always enjoy your donuts."

"And so do our customers," Nina said, starting to look fretful. "Which is why we originally came back here. We've been talking about love and Valentines. But we really came back here because we're almost out of the newest flavor."

"It's okay," Heather said, trying to stop Nina from getting as nervous as she could on occasion. "I'm just about finished with this batch. We can add them to the display case. And then I can make some more.”

“You’re not going add all of them to the display case, are you?” asked Amy, giving her friend a look reminiscent of a sad puppy dog.

“No, you can still have one,” Heather said as she put the finishing touches on the current batch.

“Thanks!” Amy said happily. “But, you know, it’s not just for my own enjoyment now. I also need to test them out to see if they would be right for Janae’s bike tour.”

"Well, if that's the excuse we're giving, then I need to have one myself," Janae joked.

"One each," Heather said. "And then we need to fill the display case. But go ahead and have a snack. Maybe it will help us all focus."

"What's this one called?" Amy asked.

Heather held up a pink and black donut proudly. "This is the Chocolate Covered Strawberries Donut."

"I think it will take me longer to say that long name than for me to

11

eat something that sounds so delicious," said Amy.

Heather chuckled and then continued with her explanation. "This is a chocolate donut that's been filled with a strawberry jam. There are two types of icing drizzled on top: dark chocolate and strawberry. Then it is topped with actual chocolate covered strawberries. Though to make it easier to bite into when it's on top of a donut, I cut the strawberries into halves before dipping them in chocolate and allowing it to solidify. I placed them all around the top of the donut. Then I added just a little more pink icing on top of the strawberries for the color."

"I don't even have to take a bite
to know that they would be
perfect for Janae's bike tours,"
said Amy. "But I'm going to take a
bite anyway."

She took a bite and then took
several more. The others joined
in, enjoying their samples.
Heather selected one as well.
She loved all her donuts, but she
thought this one really was
perfect for the Valentine's Day
crowds that were coming to her
shop as the holiday was only a
few days away. She loved the
texture of the chocolate covered
strawberries mixed with the soft
donut and smooth jelly.

"I could eat this flavor all day," Amy said. "I wanted to bring some donuts home to Jamie, but I'm afraid I'd eat them all on the way home."

Nina giggled. "They are that good. I wonder if I could make it just across the street to bring some to Nick."

"These donuts would definitely go on the tour," said Janae.

"I am glad that you all like them," said Heather. "But now we've got to get busy making more."

She gestured to where the supplies were and was about to suggest they split up to bring the finished donuts to the display case and begin making another batch. However, before she could suggest who should do what, another assistant, Digby, poked his head into the kitchen.

"Boss," Digby said. "Your friend Josie is visiting."

"Thanks," Heather said. "I guess Amy and I will bring the Chocolate Covered Strawberries Donuts that are ready out to the display case. Can you two manage here in the kitchen?"

Nina and Janae assured her that they could and began following the recipe before Heather and Amy were even out of the room.

Heather brought the donuts to the front of the shop. She and Amy started adding them to the display case, while Digby dealt with the other customers.

Josie walked up to the display case and greeted her friends.

"I was going to say love was in the air," said Josie. "But now all I can smell are these delicious donuts."

"Would you like one?" Heather asked, keeping one donut out of the display case.

"I actually came over here to tell you something, but I can't say no to one of those delightful treats," Josie said with a smile.

Heather made sure that Digby was all right at the register and then took the donut over to a table. She and Amy sat down with Josie. After accepting her praise of the new treat, Heather asked her what she wanted to talk about.

"Well," Josie said. "I just wanted to let you know that I've set a deadline for myself."

"About what?" asked Amy, who was more focused on the donut that she had grabbed than what was being discussed.

"About talking to Josh."

"You have to set a deadline about talking to your husband?" Amy asked.

Heather elbowed her friend. She knew what Josie was referring to, and Amy should have as well.

"About wanting to adopt that little boy, Nicolas," Josie explained. "I have been so nervous about bringing it up to him because I would be devastated if he said no right away. And then you gave me some good advice about there not being a perfect moment and about how this would really be a series of conversations. But I've still been nervous. However,

now I've given myself a deadline.
I need to talk to Josh about it by
Valentine's Day. That's what I've
decided."

"And you wanted to tell us to
make you accountable?" asked
Heather.

"Something like that," said Josie.

"Well, we believe in you," said
Heather. "And we know that you
and Josh would be amazing
parents. My daughter, Lilly, would
also love it if Nicolas were back in
town."

"Can I get some of those
Chocolate Covered Strawberries

Donuts to go?" asked Josie. "I think Josh would really like them."

"She does really want to be a mother," Amy joked. "She has the willpower not to eat the donuts for her significant other as she travels so he will be in a good mood for the discussion."

Heather boxed up some donuts and then handed them to her friend. Josie was about to leave but then paused.

"I almost forgot," Josie said. "I found a Valentine outside your store when I walked over here."

"It must be for Nina," Heather said, getting ready to call for her assistant.

"No. It's for you," Josie said.

She handed the card over and pointed. The red paper was folded, but the name on the front was clear. It appeared to be cut out of a newspaper and pasted onto the card, but it clearly said "Heather" and "Shepherd."

"I don't know how I feel about using cutouts from the newspaper," said Amy. "It looks a little like something a serial killer would do."

"It might also be something that a student like Lilly would make," Heather said, trying to push off those concerns.

However, when she saw the message inside, she immediately became concerned that Amy was right. Inside was written: I'm going to kill you.

Chapter 2 – Cupid Concerns

It took Heather a moment to react after seeing the threat. Amy and Josie looked at her, concerned, but she didn't know what to say for a moment. Heather had certainly faced danger before when she started investigating crimes, and she had even been threatened before. However, she didn't expect threats to arrive at her business. They also weren't usually so cut and dry. It was very difficult to come up with an alternate meaning for "I'm going to kill you."

"Heather, what's wrong?" Josie asked.

"Did Ryan say something really scandalous?" Amy joked, referring to Heather's husband. "Did it take your breath away?"

"I wish," Heather said finally. "This note isn't nearly so nice."

She showed the two women what was inside the Valentine because she didn't want to read it aloud. Josie immediately turned pale.

"Oh no. I'm so sorry I brought this inside. I would never have given it to you if I knew. What do we do? Are you in danger?"

"No one is going to hurt Heather while I'm around," Amy said with an air of bravado.

"Thank you," Heather said.
"Seeing this did frighten me for a
moment, but maybe that was all
its intention."

"What do you mean?" Josie
asked, wringing her hands.

"I mean maybe there is nothing to
this threat," said Heather. "Maybe
the sender has no intention of
hurting me. Maybe he just
wanted to scare me."

"Do you really think so?" asked
Josie.

"That's most likely," Heather
agreed. "If someone really

wanted to kill me, they wouldn't announce it."

"That's right," said Amy. "Killers don't act like villains in superhero movies."

"Why don't you bring those donuts back to Josh and focus on the potential adoption?" said Heather.

Josie still looked unsure. "You promise that you'll be careful?"

"I promise," said Heather.

Josie was eventually persuaded to leave and continue with her original plans. Once she was gone, Amy gave Heather a serious look.

"Do you really think this threat is no big deal?" she asked. "Or did you just not want to worry Josie?"

"I'm not sure," said Heather. "I think I should tell Ryan and his partner, Detective Peters, about the threat just in case. That is, unless we can determine who it was from right away."

"What do you mean?" asked Amy. "You know who wants to kill you?"

"No. Not kill me," said Heather. "But we do know someone who likes to cause trouble for the shop and who might be annoyed about his nephew sneaking over here to give my assistant Valentines."

"Mr. Rankle?"

"I think it's worth having a conversation with him," Heather agreed.

Heather checked that her assistants would be all right without her for a little while, and then headed across the street with Amy to Sun and Fun Novelties. Nina's sweetheart, Nick, greeted them as soon as they entered.

"Hi, Heather and Amy," he said. "What brings you over here? You didn't figure out the clues that I gave to Nina already, did you? I was hoping it would last longer and be fun for her to guess what our date would be."

"You don't have to worry about that," Amy said. "We found something else that we need to investigate."

"What's that?" asked Nick.

"Is Mr. Rankle around?" asked Heather.

"That can't be the mystery. He's almost always here," Nick said. However, he went to the back room and called for his uncle to come out.

Mr. Rankle appeared, looking as he always did when he saw the bakers – annoyed. He leaned on his cane and glared at them.

Heather thought that they had been making some progress in their neighborly relations recently after she and Amy helped him and his beau with some investigations. However, he certainly didn't look at them with a friendly look.

"What do you want?" he asked by way of a greeting.

"We'll cut right to the chase too," Amy said. "Did you send Heather a Valentine?"

"Why would I send her a
Valentine?" asked Mr. Rankle as
if it were the most ridiculous thing
in the world.

"It wasn't a very nice Valentine,"
said Heather. "And last year, you
did think that those Valentines
you were receiving were a prank
from us until you learned that you
really did have a secret admirer."

"Nick is the one around here who
sends Valentines," Mr. Rankle
said as Nick blushed. "Not me."

"So, you never sent Heather a
threat?" Amy pushed.

"No," Mr. Rankle said. "After how you helped Ethel, I would never threaten you. I might not like you or your gross desserts, but I wouldn't threaten you. I've even, almost, gotten accustomed to sharing the same street as you."

"Thanks," Heather said, knowing this was as close to a compliment as they might ever get from Mr. Rankle.

"Of course. But others might have some trouble with your being here. After all," Mr. Rankle shrugged, "it used to be a quiet island. Then you started tripping over dead bodies all the time."

Heather was about to protest. She was constantly explaining to her neighbor how she didn't cause murders to happen. She just investigated them when they did happen.

"There might be others who don't share the same feelings that I do," Mr. Rankle said. "Who might not feel as kindly as I do."

"If you're the kind one, then we really are in trouble," said Amy, shaking her head.

Chapter 3 – The Police Station

Heather and Amy often visited the Key West Police Station. They went there when they were assisting with investigations and to bring donuts to Heather's husband and his fellow officers. However, today Heather felt funny about visiting there.

She wasn't sure what to make of the threat she had received. Part of her thought she was overreacting to it. After all, she couldn't understand why a killer would tell her that he was about to attack. That would give her time to prepare and protect herself. It was most likely a prank, and she felt guilty wasting police time on a matter like that.

On the other hand, if she really was being threatened, it would be unwise to ignore the matter. If one of her friends had been threatened, she would advise them to seek protection. She also had to consider her friends and family. She had a twelve-year-old daughter. If there was a chance that the threat-sender could come after her at home, she needed to take action. She couldn't let Lilly and those she cared about be in potential danger too.

"Is everything all right?" Ryan asked when he saw Heather and Amy walk toward his desk.

"No," Amy said at the same time
that Heather answered, "I'm not
sure."

"What is it?" he asked, pulling his
wife into a hug.

"I received a Valentine today,"
said Heather.

"Should I be jealous?" he asked,
trying to ease some tension.

"You should be worried," said
Amy. "Show him, Heather."

She brought out the Valentine
and showed it to Ryan. He looked
at it gravely.

"Josie found it outside Donut
Delights and brought it in. It was
very busy today, and I was in the
kitchen most of the morning,"
said Heather. "No one noticed it
being left there."

"Should we be scared?" asked
Amy.

"I'm going to treat this very
seriously," Ryan said. "But it most
likely is someone pulling a prank
in bad taste. We get a lot of
people doing crazy things around
Valentine's Day. Heather is a bit
of a minor celebrity now.
Someone might have chosen to
harass her because of their failed
romances around the holiday."

"I'm not a minor celebrity,"
Heather protested.

"In Key West you might be," said
Amy. "Hope does write articles in
the local paper about all the
murders you solve. We make
sure that she doesn't include
pictures and we do try to avoid
the limelight. But your name is
still in the paper."

"And that's what this looks like to
me," said Ryan, indicating the
name on the front of the card.
"Both of the words Heather and
Shepherd are complete. They're
not made out of individual letters.
They were printed as full words,
and someone cut them out."

"Do you think it was from the local paper and that my name was taken right from there?" asked Heather. "Or do you think the sender found the words they needed? Heather is a common name. And Shepherd could also be referring to the job where someone takes care of sheep."

"I'm not sure," Ryan said. "But we will look into this. I'll check this for fingerprints first."

"Josie's prints are bound to be all over it," said Heather. "She didn't know that this was going to be a piece of evidence. I touched it too."

"It's still possible that the sender left their own prints and we can find them."

"Hi, Heather! Hi, Amy."

They turned and saw Detective Peters walking toward them. He was a young officer but was proving himself as very capable. He grinned when he saw them.

"Are you here delivering some donuts? I bet you have some really great new flavors for Valentine's Day. I'll probably want to give some to my girlfriend, Hope, too."

"You might want to contact her," Amy said. "Our new case might relate to her newspaper stories."

"We have a new case?" Detective Peters asked, hurrying closer.

"We do now," said Ryan.

"What sort of case?" asked Peters.

"A threat was made against Heather," said Ryan. "And I would like to know by whom."

He showed the Valentine to Peters, who looked nervous.

"That does look like what appears in the *Key West, Key News*," he said. "And I don't like what was written."

"Me neither," Heather agreed.

"We'll check for fingerprints and then canvass the area," said Ryan. "Maybe someone saw the note delivered."

"We can have officers patrol your neighborhood tonight if you think it would help," said Peters. "The good news is that you have a very good security system at your house already."

"And a guard dog," Heather joked. She loved her small, white, mixed-breed dog, Dave, very much. He had protected her before, but it was still funny to think of the goofy pup as an actual guard dog.

"Don't worry," Ryan said. "I know, in general, you're perfectly capable of looking out for yourself. But we all care about you and are pretty good at what we do too. We're not going to let this threat come true."

"Never a dull moment," Amy lamented. "Some people get poetry in their Valentine's Day cards. Heather gets threats!"

Chapter 4 – Overreacting

Heather slept fitfully that night. She didn't like that an anonymous threat could hold such sway over her activities, but she did feel nervous.

After her visit to the police station, she had returned to Donut Delights with Amy, Ryan, and Detective Peters. She made sure that her staff was still holding up well, but she didn't want to worry them. They made some inquiries about whether anyone saw the note being left by the donut shop, but it yielded no results. They visited Josie at J+J's, the restaurant that she and Josh now ran and owned, and she gave them her fingerprints to compare to what was found on the card.

Heather went home and spent the evening inside her locked home. Her daughter, beloved pets, and their good friends/neighbors, Eva and Leila, kept her company. She was grateful that they showed their love, but she felt like she was putting on an act all night, pretending like she was not concerned about the note. She didn't want to worry them when she didn't know how serious it was.

When Ryan returned home, he reported that only Josie's and Heather's fingerprints were on the card, so that was a dead end in their investigation.

As Heather tried to sleep that night, she had the unhappy thought that there was little more that they could do to determine who wrote the threat – that is, unless the writer took steps to act upon what he said he would do and kill Heather. It was hard to stay calm when she knew she could find the person only if they were actively trying to kill her.

The next morning, Heather drank more coffee than usual to wake herself up and clear her head. Ryan had driven Lilly to school, rationalizing that she would be safer riding in a police cruiser than a bus. He would alert the school about what was happening with their family so there was no chance that someone could try and use Lilly to get to Heather.

Heather sipped her coffee as she tried to figure out what to do with her day. She had planned on making donuts for all the Valentine's Day orders. Should she still go ahead with that? Part of her worried that she would be a sitting duck if she followed her usual routine. She also might be putting her assistants and customers in danger. However, the other part of her didn't want to sit around all day, worrying about what might happen and not go outside. She didn't want this threat to stop her from living her life.

Dave sat next to her as she drank from her mug, and she pet his fur. She found it reassuring.

"Thanks for the support, Dave," Heather said. "I hope you're not just doing it for a donut."

He barked, which she took to mean that he really did love her donuts, but that he was there for her out of love and not hunger. She decided that this deserved a reward as well as anything and found him a portion of donut that didn't have chocolate in it. His chomping on the donut caused the family kitten, Cupcake, to barge into the room and demand a snack too. Heather gave in. She was willing to show those she loved how much she cared.

A knock at the door startled her, but Dave wasn't barking in alarm so she realized that it must be someone that she knew arriving there. She checked and saw that Amy had come down from her home on the top floor to see her friend. Heather let her inside quickly.

"You look like you didn't get any sleep at all," Amy said.

"That's close to the truth," said Heather.

"I didn't sleep well either," Amy admitted. "Jamie was also nervous about this threat. You know, after everything that happened when he had that stalker. We spent a good portion of the night staring out the window, making sure everything looked normal."

"I'm sorry you felt you had to do that," Heather said. "I really hate that this is happening."

"Well, let's have some of the donuts I know you hide in your house and we can figure out what we want to do today."

Amy headed toward the kitchen and greeted Dave and Cupcake. Then she grabbed a Chocolate Covered Strawberries Donut.

"Did I mention that this donut was amazing?" Amy asked. "Maybe it was a competitor on the island who sent that note? Trying to stop you from making such amazing donuts that everyone wants to buy."

"Maybe that was who did it," said Heather with a nod. "They don't really want to kill me. They just want to slow my business down. And if that's the case, then I can't let them succeed in their plan."

"What are you saying?"

"I'm saying I can't let this threat stop me from living my life and running my business," said Heather. "After I finish my coffee and you finish that donut, we're going to Donut Delights. I'm going to do what my plan for the day originally was."

"Great," said Amy. "After coffee and donuts, we can make coffee and donuts."

Heather laughed and was feeling better now that a decision was made. She was starting to feel like they had all been overreacting to the note. It must have been a prank or a competitor trying to ruin some business for her. No one really planned on killing her.

She and Amy got ready quickly and headed toward Donut Delights. Heather noticed that their usual produce delivery truck was partially visible behind the shop as she walked toward the front door. She thought this was odd because usually supplies arrived early in the morning. However, she continued inside to make sure her employees were all right.

It was extremely busy inside with a line of customers that Digby and Janae were dealing with.

"Heather," Janae called. "We're glad you're here. Nina and Luz are baking donuts constantly, but it still feels like we're behind with customers in the shop and online orders."

"I'll go straight to the kitchen," Heather said. Amy was at her heels as they followed through with what she said.

When she reached the kitchen, she saw that Nina and Luz were working quickly, making different donuts to fill the orders.

"What do you need me to do?" Heather asked.

"We really need some more of the Chocolate Covered Strawberries Donuts," Nina said. "But we need more strawberries, and our fruit delivery hasn't arrived yet."

"Really?" asked Heather. "Well, I saw it outside, so it's here now. They just must be running late because so many restaurants need things for romantic meals."

"It's here?" asked Nina. "Well, that's good. We've been running around all morning. We didn't notice. The delivery person normally comes right in."

Heather nodded. She looked toward the door, waiting to see if someone was about to enter. When there were no signs of it, she went to the door herself.

She walked out the back door and looked around. Then she gasped.

Amy ran toward her. "What is it?"

Heather pointed. A woman in a delivery uniform who had red hair just like Heather's was lying dead next to her truck.

"There's been a murder," Heather said quietly. "And I don't think we were overreacting to that note now."

Chapter 5 – Crime Scene

Heather hated seeing the back of Donut Delights roped off as a crime scene. However, she hated the reason for it even more. She couldn't believe that a delivery driver had been killed right outside her shop. She also couldn't help feeling somewhat responsible for what happened.

Her assistants were also feeling glum. Donut Delights was closed to the public while the police investigated, but the assistants were all still at the shop. Heather was waiting inside the kitchen with them.

Ryan had said that they should close so no new customers could come by and contaminate the scene. However, since it was clear that the delivery driver never made it inside the shop, they could continue baking donuts for their online and currently reserved orders. Her assistants were making the donuts to keep busy as they waited to give statements.

Nina looked especially troubled, and Heather pulled her to the side.

"I just can't believe that we didn't know this happened," Nina said sadly. "She was right outside, and we were so busy that we didn't notice. What if there was something we could have done?"

"Don't drive yourself crazy with this," Heather said, giving her a hug. "You were at work, baking. There's nothing to reproach yourself for. The only person who should feel guilty is the person who actually murdered this poor woman."

Nina nodded and looked a little more at ease as she went back to mixing frosting. Heather just wished that she could take her own advice. She knew that the killer was the person really responsible for this tragedy. However, Heather couldn't help thinking that the victim was killed because the killer mistook the delivery person for her.

She tried not to dwell on this
because she knew it wasn't
helpful in solving the case.
However, it was hard to push
these feelings of guilt and fear for
her own safety aside. Luckily,
Amy soon came to give her some
news.

"Ryan said we can go out and
examine the scene with him
now," Amy reported. "He and
Peters combed the area, and
there's no one nearby waiting to
come out and hurt you."

"The killer must think that he
already succeeded," said
Heather.

Amy chose not to respond to that and instead said, "The medical examiner is just about done too. He should be able to tell us what killed her."

Heather bit back a comment about how what had really gotten her killed was her hair color and that she worked close to Donut Delights. Instead, she just followed Amy outside and met the detectives and medical examiner.

"I'm sorry we didn't catch the person who wrote that threat before this happened," Ryan said when he saw her, echoing what they were all thinking.

"Everyone did a great job at keeping me secure," Heather said. "We hadn't considered that the threat writer might make a mistake like this."

"Her hair is exactly the same color as yours," Amy said. "And you do have similar body types."

"What's her name?" Heather asked Ryan. "She was new to the route. I only met her once when she dropped off produce, and I didn't catch her name. I didn't even think that someone might mistake her for me."

"Her name is Bonnie Purvis," said Ryan. "She lived and worked on the island. We contacted her

employer, the produce company.
She's worked with them for a
long time. They always thought
she was conscientious and when
I contacted them, they said that
they were starting to get worried
about her. She's not normally late
and usually answers her radio.
She's been on this particular
route for about a month now. She
changed to it because the hours
were better."

"Do we know what time she
arrived here?" asked Heather.

"The company said that they
were backed up because of how
large many restaurants' orders
had been recently. However, she

should have arrived here around eight a.m.," said Ryan.

"That is a busy time inside the shop," said Heather. "I'm not surprised my employees didn't notice a van outside."

"And customers probably thought it was business as usual," Amy added.

"But this also means that the van was here for about an hour until you arrived," said Peters.

"The killer probably got to her soon after she arrived," Heather said. "Otherwise, she would have been able to tell my assistants she was here and bring in the packages."

"And now we've got to ask what it was that killed her," said Amy. "We saw some blood on the ground, but we couldn't see the wound. She was lying face down."

"She was shot in the chest," Ryan said. "After the autopsy is performed, we might learn more about the bullet and gun that was used. However, we do know that she was shot with a gun from a few feet away."

"This poor woman," was all Heather could say.

"Yeah," Amy agreed. "This is much worse than being shot with one of Cupid's arrows."

Chapter 6 – Promising Justice

The investigators searched all over the crime scene, but there didn't seem to be much to go on at first glance. There were some pieces of trash that were found out back, but they more likely fell out of one of the businesses' garbage cans than were trapped by the killer. They questioned the neighbors, but no one seemed to notice anything unusual at that time (though Mr. Rankle did have some cranky comments for them.)

Heather's friend, Bernadette, who ran the bookshop down the street, had installed some security cameras, but they didn't pick up anyone headed toward the donut shop.

There didn't seem to be any evidence that the killer had been onboard the delivery van at any point. After checking the inventory log, they discovered there was nothing missing from the van. The killer probably surprised the driver when she was walking toward Donut Delights.

Heather was feeling discouraged. She still felt like they had no solid leads on how to discover the person behind these crimes, but now the criminal had actually escalated to murder.

To make matters worse, the victim's husband was due to come to the police station at any moment, and Heather wasn't sure she could face him. After searching the scene, Heather and Amy had returned to the Key West Police Station with Ryan and Peters.

Chief Chet had graciously volunteered to inform the spouse about his wife's death so the investigators could spend more time at the crime scene. He hated when murders occurred on his island. He also had a soft spot for Heather and her donuts and wanted to make sure that she wouldn't become a victim too. He wanted the investigators to be able to do their work at the crime scene. However, he had asked the husband to come in when he felt up to it to make a statement. Bill Purvis had just called to inform them he was on his way.

Heather was trying to remain calm. She kept telling herself that she wasn't responsible for this woman's death. Someone was out to get her, so Heather was a victim in all this too. However, she still felt responsible emotionally. Maybe if she'd done more to catch the threat writer earlier, he wouldn't have had time to act. She should have remembered that there was a delivery driver with hair similar to hers and warned her of potential danger.

"Stop," Amy said.

"What?" Heather asked, getting knocked out of her thoughts.

"I told you to stop," Amy repeated.

"Stop what?" asked Heather. "I'm not doing anything."

"It might not look like you're doing anything. It might look like you're just sitting here, waiting for news. But I'm your best friend, and I know you. I know what you're really doing," Amy said. "You're blaming yourself for what happened."

"I'm not," Heather said, trying to protest. "It's like I told Nina. Only the person who killed this woman is to blame."

"I know that you're saying that out loud," said Amy. "But I'm not really sure you believe it. I just hope you're not torturing yourself. Because it's really not your fault. All you did was receive an evil Valentine. And if you keep blaming yourself, it will stop you from thinking clearly and solving this case."

"I know. But it's difficult," Heather said finally.

"We need to be at the top of our game," Amy said. "We need to get justice for this lady who was just in the wrong place at the wrong time. And we need to catch this guy before he realizes his mistake and comes after you."

Heather nodded. "You're right."

She felt more resolved after she had this conversation with her friend. However, she still did take Ryan up on his offer where she wouldn't talk to the victim's husband face to face.

When Bill Purvis arrived, Ryan and Detective Peters led him into the interrogation room to make his statement. Heather and Amy stood on the other side of the two-way mirror, watching the conversation.

"Do you think he'll have anything helpful to tell us?" asked Amy.

Heather shrugged. "If the killer was really after me, then he might not. But it is always useful to hear about the victim's life to see if it impacted their death."

The two women listened as Bill Purvis recounted how happy his wife was with her new route because she got to come home earlier, but how sad he was that now she wouldn't be coming home at all. He couldn't think of any enemies that she might have had, and she never mentioned any troubles at work.

After taking his statement and thanking him for his time, Ryan and Peters began to lead him out of the room. Heather and Amy started to walk away, but they weren't fast enough getting out of Bill Purvis's line of sight.

"Bonnie?" he called.

Heather turned to face him, trying to hide how uncomfortable she felt.

"I'm sorry," Bill said. "I know they just told me about what happened to Bonnie, but when I saw that hair… I still thought it was my wife for a moment. You look so much like her."

"She really does?" asked Amy.

"Well, the hair is just the same," Bill said. "And from behind, they look just alike. Same height. I know my wife's face, of course. And I see the differences. But there are a lot of similarities too. You do look very much alike."

"I'm very sorry for your loss," Heather said. "And I'm sorry if I caused you any more undue stress because of my appearance."

"It's not your fault," Bill Purvis said. "But the resemblance is striking. Is that why you're here? Are you going to set some sort of trap to catch whoever went after my Bonnie?"

"I am going to help the police with their investigation," Heather said. "And I promise that we will get justice for your wife."

"I believe you," he said. "Coming from someone who looks like she could be Bonnie's relative, this means a lot."

Chapter 7 – Digging Up the Past

"I'm sure," Heather said.

"But are you really sure?" asked Amy.

"Yes. I don't have a long-lost sister," Heather repeated, trying to get her friend off this train of thought. Amy seemed to think it was fascinating to imagine Heather's unknown distant relative popping up on the island.

"But if she were lost…?" Amy started.

"It is possible that she's distantly related somehow," Heather admitted. "But I know all my immediate relations. And if she's a distant relative and I never knew about her, I don't see what bearing that could have on the case."

"I guess that's right," said Amy.

The two women had returned to Heather's house and turned on the alarm system. They were sitting at the kitchen table, eating some leftover donuts and thinking about the case. Dave and Cupcake were close by to offer moral support – and beg for donut pieces.

"Your donuts are always good," Amy said, picking up a vanilla one. "But I do wish you had more of those Chocolate Covered Strawberries Donuts here.”

“Me too,” said Heather. “But I needed to use what we had at the shop to fill orders and not bring them home with me. I had to send Luz out to get some more fresh strawberries from the store because our produce order is now evidence.”

“They’ll take care of all the orders that were made,” Amy assured her. “Your other location in Texas can pick up the slack for online orders if need be, but I think everyone working at the shop can handle it. The only problem is that they’re worried about you now.”

"I'm worried about them too," said Heather. "But the shop is still closed to the public for now so the killer can't just walk inside. And Ryan said more police would be stationed on the street. An officer is going to escort Janae home when it's closing time because she has red hair too. I offered to let her go home early, but she didn't want to leave the others."

"I think Janae will be safe," Amy said. "You both have red hair, but you don't look much alike otherwise. She's a good deal younger than us. She's taller. And she's a professional cyclist. She looks like an athlete. And we…well, most of the exercise we do is running around the bakery or chasing killers."

Heather laughed. "I guess that's true. And yes, I believe my assistants will be safe. I just don't like the thought of someone with a vendetta against me free on the streets. He's already killed one innocent person. What if he makes another mistake?"

"We can't let that happen," said Amy.

Dave barked in agreement.

Heather nodded. "But now we need to figure out what our next move is."

"Well," Amy said, thinking about it. "Are we sure the killer was after you?"

"Pretty sure," said Heather. "I was sent a threatening note saying someone wanted to kill me and then someone who looked just like me who was near my place of business was murdered. I think someone is out to get me."

"She didn't look just like you," Amy clarified.

"Are you going to say that she was younger and skinnier again too?" Heather asked, trying to make a joke to lighten the tension.

"No. Just now that I've seen a picture of her, I don't think you look exactly alike. Same hair and build, but your faces are different. You'd probably be long-lost cousins and not sisters if I think about it."

"We're not long-lost anything."

"Okay, fine. I'm getting off topic anyway. My point was going to be that if we think the killer is after you—"

"And we do."

"Then, we need to figure out who is your enemy," Amy said simply. "You're my best friend, and I don't like thinking about this. But if someone wants to kill you, there has to be a reason."

Heather tapped the table as she thought. "I can't think of any enemies in my personal life. And while I think a competitor on the island might be willing to try and scare me to sabotage my business, I can't see any of them committing murder for chocolate sales. So then, it needs to be related to our sleuthing work."

"I was thinking the same thing," Amy agreed.

"We can have Ryan check and see if anyone we sent to prison was released early," Heather said. "But I think that because most of the people we caught were guilty of murder, they should be in jail for a long time."

"Maybe it wasn't the killer who is out to get you," Amy said. "What if it was someone else who was affected by the case? A family member who doesn't like that their loved one is in jail and is blaming the wrong person. You."

"There could be something to that," said Heather. "I had an incident like that when I lived in Texas. Some information they didn't want to be uncovered came out during the course of my investigation. They blamed me."

"We'll have to go through our old cases and see if anything raises a red flag."

"There is something I've been thinking about," Heather admitted. "An old case where some people involved still live on the island. And I thought of it because of the newspaper clippings that were used on the Valentine. But…"

"But what?"

"Well, I don't really think it could be her."

"Her who?"

"Hope Penwell," Heather said. "We considered her a suspect in another case. And we know how she loves a good story for the paper."

"There were also some times that we thought she was obsessed with us," Amy agreed with a nod.

"But we've worked with her on some cases since then, and she doesn't seem like a killer. She's almost a friend now."

"But we need to treat this case objectively," said Amy. "We have some reasons to consider her a suspect. We shouldn't ignore them."

"I guess you're right. And it wouldn't hurt to talk to her."

"Well, as long as Detective Peters doesn't find out you might be accusing his girlfriend of murder!"

Chapter 8 – Suspecting Hope

"I'm having second thoughts," Amy said as she followed Heather into the newspaper office.

"Me too," Heather admitted.

She had felt good about having someone to ask questions to instead of sitting at home and fearing that a killer was coming after her. However, now that they were at the office, Heather felt even more conflicted.

Their relationship with Hope had started off very strained. They met her when the Key West Santa Claus was being accused of murder, and they needed details on the story she wrote. They had considered her a suspect for a while because she had information about the gifts that could have allowed her to disguise the poisoned package as just another Christmas present. However, they eventually discovered that it was someone else who had committed the crime.

Hope was always on the lookout for a good scoop for the paper and had persistently (and somewhat annoyingly) asked to do stories on Heather and Amy that they refused. However, she also knew when to keep a story quiet if it would cause a killer to do something dangerous that could affect people in town. She shared information with them when needed. It was also clear that Detective Peters cared about her very much, and that she felt the same way about him. She couldn't be the killer, could she?

Hope walked into the room and grinned when she saw the pair.

"Hello there!" she said, running toward them. "I was just debating whether to track you down or not."

"Track us down?" Amy asked nervously. "Why? What did you want? What are you going to do with Heather?"

"I'm going to question her," Hope said, not quite understanding Amy's panic. "There was a murder that occurred behind your donut shop, wasn't there? That's why the shop is closed today?"

"That's right," Heather said.

"I was hoping you could give me some comments for the paper," Hope said. "Any chance that's why you're here? Or is this part of your investigation?"

"Do you mind if we speak privately?" asked Heather.

Hope looked a little worried but showed them to a room where they could speak. They all sat down. Heather had a moment where she considered that Hope's anxious expression might be due to a guilty conscience. However, the first thing that Hope asked brushed these thoughts away.

"Is he okay?"

"Who?" asked Amy.

"Miguel. Detective Peters," Hope said, clarifying. "Is that why we need to talk privately? Did something happen to him? I haven't spoken to him since this morning when he said he had an important case to work on."

"Peters is fine," Heather said quickly, and Hope seemed to relax visibly.

"Then, what's going on?" asked Hope.

"What time did you speak to Peters?" asked Heather.

"Around nine, I guess," said Hope, thinking. "Yes. Because it was right before a pancake brunch fundraiser that I was covering, and that was going to start at nine thirty."

"You were already at this fundraiser?" asked Amy.

"Yes," said Hope. "I was there at eight because they wanted to tell me about all the special syrup flavors before the guests arrived. But why are you so interested in my morning? Does this have to do with the murder? *Did you think of me as a suspect?*"

"No," Heather and Amy said. However, it was said a little too quickly and in unison to be believed.

"I thought we were friends," Hope said.

"I thought we were just potential subjects in a story," Amy muttered.

"We are friends," Heather said instead. "And we didn't really think you were the killer. It's just that something related back to the newspaper, so we had to be sure."

Hope stopped looking miffed and looked curious. "Something about the murder relates to the paper? All I know so far is that the murder occurred outside of your shop and it was the delivery driver that was the victim."

"I'll tell you more, but it has to be off the record for now," said Heather. "But you can have the story once it's been solved. But we can't have all the information revealed to the public right now."

"Yeah," Amy said, stressing how serious this was. "It could be very dangerous for Heather and her family."

"It's a deal," said Hope. "I won't write anything now."

"I received a Valentine in the mail that said someone wanted to kill me. And the woman who was killed had the same hair as me and was targeted right outside my shop."

"So, the killer meant to get you?" asked Hope.

"Yes. We think so," said Heather.

"But what does this have to do with the paper?"

"The threat was written with words cut out from a newspaper. Ryan thought it looked like it came from the *Key West, Key News.* And we agree," said Heather.

"I'll look at it, and I can tell you for certain," Hope said. "But I don't think anyone here would be out to get you. The only one who would is still safely behind bars."

"Then, you think it was most likely someone who receives the paper and isn't an employee," said Heather.

"That's not going to make our job any easier," Amy said.

"I'm afraid not," Hope said, not able to keep the pride out of her voice. "We have quite a substantial number of readers."

Chapter 9 – Smoking Gun Cases

"Well, that was a bust," Amy said.

"No. It wasn't," Heather said. "We probably should have had more faith in Hope from the get-go."

"That's quite a phrase," Amy joked. "Faith in Hope."

Heather let out a laugh. The two women were leaving the newspaper office and headed toward Amy's car. They checked it to make sure that no one had tampered with anything, just to be cautious, before climbing inside it.

"But it was good that we checked out that newspaper lead," said Heather. "It could have been possible that Hope was harboring a grudge."

"And just using poor Peters to get insight into how to pull off the perfect crime?" asked Amy. "That would have been cold."

"But she has an alibi for the time of the murder," said Heather. "She can't be the killer. And it's useful to know that it's unlikely that anyone at the paper could be involved."

"How is that useful?" asked Amy. "Maybe we eliminated a dozen people. But now there are hundreds of readers on the island. I guess I'll have faith in Eva and Leila and say that even though they read the paper, they can't be guilty. So two less than hundreds of suspects."

"Now we can focus on other leads," said Heather. "I've been trying to think of cases we cracked that involved guns."

"But if the guns were the murder weapon in a case, then they were either taken into evidence or were destroyed," said Amy. "The killer shouldn't have been able to use it to try and kill you."

"Not that specific gun," said Heather. "But it is possible that the killer chose this weapon because that was the weapon that was used in a different case. It's symbolic."

"Like if you solved a murder where the weapon was poisoned jelly and sent the killer to jail for life, then his son might try to poison you with poisoned jelly as well?" asked Amy.

"Exactly. But with a gun instead of food," said Heather. "I know it's possible that this isn't related. But it might be. And this allows us to narrow down our past cases based on certain criteria."

"I guess that's good," said Amy. "After all, we've solved over sixty

cases just since we moved to
Key West."

"What were some of our cases
that involved guns?" Heather
asked aloud. "There was one
used in the Sleepy Hollow case,
but I can't imagine someone from
there traveling all the way here
for a grudge."

"A gun was the murder weapon
for a cruise case we solved," said
Amy, looking dreamy. "That was
the night Jamie proposed to me.
All it took was for a crazed killer
wielding a weapon to finally get
him to pop the question."

"He'd been carrying that
engagement ring around with him

for weeks waiting for the right moment to ask," Heather said.

"I love that guy," said Amy. "But to get back on task – I don't know if that case could relate to someone hating you. Everyone on the ship was grateful for what we did."

Heather kept thinking about her past cases. As she thought about all the means of violence that she had encountered, part of her was amazed that she hadn't been in danger like this before. She tried to think of other cases with similarities to this one.

Finally, she said, "What about the holiday pageant?"

"The one Digby directed?" asked Amy.

"Right. Digby took over as the director after the previous one was murdered," Heather reminded her. "The original director was shot with a gun and then bludgeoned to death."

"Not one of our most pleasant crime scenes," Amy said. "And weren't threatening notes a part of that crime too?"

Heather nodded. "We caught the killer and the note writer. But maybe someone else involved in this case didn't like what we did."

"It's worth checking out," Amy said, revving the engine. "But who do we talk to first?"

***

"I know more about those children than I ever wanted to know!" Amy said.

Heather sighed. Visiting the parents involved with the holiday pageant hadn't revealed much. They had found out a lot about the children's schoolwork and extracurricular activities since winter break had ended. However, they didn't find anyone who had a motive for killing Heather after she caught the director's murderer.

The parents all seemed grateful to her for solving the case and allowing the show to go on. They talked to the adult actors in the show and got a similar response. No one seemed to bear her any ill will for her part in the proceedings. In fact, most were happy to see her and thank her in person. Even the man they had considered their prime suspect for a while was glad to see them and explain how all stolen property from the case had been reunited with its owner.

Heather had even gained some extra business. Her visits to question those involved in the pageant had also led to some people making Valentine's Day orders with her. Since her shop had lost out on walk-in business that day while it was closed as a crime scene, she was happy to take the orders.

However, now they felt like they were back to square one with the case.

"I don't know what to do," Amy said. "The cases we looked into don't seem related to this threat on your life now. And we just don't have time to go through every single case you've ever investigated. You have too impressive a resume to do that."

"Thanks," said Heather. "But there must be something that we can do to narrow down what cases to look at."

"Any ideas on what they could be?"

"Not right now," Heather admitted. "But maybe an idea will occur to me after a good night's sleep. After all the legwork we did today, I'm *exhausted*. Even with the fear that someone is after me, I know I'll sleep well tonight!"

Chapter 10 – Back to Work

The next afternoon, Heather sat at a table looking out the window of Donut Delights. She imagined this must have been what Amy and Jamie were doing when they kept a lookout from home the night the threat had first appeared. She was trying to relax, but it was difficult.

She had finally gotten some sleep last night due to pure exhaustion. However, the morning had been stressful. Donut Delights had been allowed to open for normal business again (though the area behind the shop was still roped off as a crime scene). Heather thought it might be slow because customers might be hesitant to buy food so close to where a murder had occurred. However, the opposite seemed to be true. Customers must have learned that the crime happened outside the shop and wouldn't affect the donuts. They were flocking to the store to stock up on their Valentine's Day treats and to hear whatever gossip they could about the grisly crime.

Heather had spent the morning in the kitchen creating Chocolate Covered Strawberries Donuts with the fruit they had picked themselves. She had started at the counter but found herself jumping every time the door opened. She didn't think that was helpful and relegated herself to the kitchen. She had always found baking donuts soothing, and the activity did help her.

When they reached their usual afternoon lull, Heather headed to the front of the shop to sit down. She kept an eye on people walking by as she sipped a coffee. So far, she hadn't noticed anything suspicious, but she did notice something sweet. She could see Mr. Rankle standing outside his shop and glaring at them. At first, she thought that he was giving her the evil eye because another murder had happened in town and he thought she was bad luck. However, then she saw that he and Nick were alternating this position through the day. Mr. Rankle and Nick were doing their own version of a neighborhood watch and were keeping an eye on the donut shop.

She smiled, realizing that even in the most troubled times, there were people who were willing to help. Her smile grew as she saw Amy approaching.

Amy entered the shop and plopped down at the table with Heather. Janae put some Chocolate Covered Strawberries Donuts in front of them without being asked. Heather thanked her, and Amy grabbed a donut right away. It wasn't until she had finished eating her first donut and Janae had returned to the counter that Amy commented on the headwear of all the assistants.

"What's on Janae's head? And everyone else's for that matter?"

"Valentine's Day hats," Heather answered.

"Is this your asserting your power as a boss and making them wear ridiculous things? I notice you're not wearing one," said Amy.

"They're wearing them because I thought Janae should hide her hair and I needed a reason for them all to wear something. I thought hats with hearts on them were a festive excuse," said Heather. "But I want to make certain that no one else is confused with me and becomes a target."

Amy looked uncomfortable. "I like that you're trying to protect everyone. But you better protect yourself too."

"I'm not taking any unnecessary risks," Heather assured her friend. "But I think the best thing we can do for my safety is solve this case."

Amy nodded and pulled her tablet out of her purse. "I brought the tablet like you said. All our notes from previous cases are on here. But remember, there are a lot of them."

"I know," said Heather. "But until we have new a way of narrowing down what cases might be related to this one, we'll just have to examine all of them. Maybe reviewing all our notes will help us realize who might have a deadly grudge against me."

Amy turned on the tablet, and they began looking through the case notes. It was slow work because they needed to reacquaint themselves with all the pieces of particular cases and they occasionally needed to decipher Amy's peculiar abbreviations.

Heather was happy to take a break when Josh and Josie entered the donut shop. She waved as they came in and they joined her at the table.

"How are you holding up?" Josie asked.

"As well as can be expected," said Heather. "But I know that Lilly has protection at school, so I feel relieved about that."

"This situation makes me so mad," Josh said. "I don't like anyone threatening my friends. If I ever come across this creep, I'm going to hit him with one of my frying pans.”

“I also want to catch the person responsible and send them to jail,” said Heather. “I hate that the poor delivery driver was caught up in this.”

“I know you’ll catch them,” Josie said. “But please promise that you’ll be careful as you sleuth. We couldn’t stand it if anything happened to you.”

“I promise I’ll be careful,” Heather agreed. “And we’re not doing any dangerous work right now. All we’re doing is going through old case files to see if anyone sticks out as a potential suspect.”

"You made friends with the work you do. Like how you cleared me of a charge when I was really innocent," Josh said. "But I guess you made some enemies too."

Heather didn't want to dwell on this with her friends, so she tried changing the subject.

"I'm surprised to see you both here at this time of day."

"The lunch rush hasn't quite kicked in," said Josh. "And my assistant, Kate, is running things right now. She's doing a great job. She's really grown into the position."

"And she insisted that we check on you," said Josie. "She cares about you too. It's really because of you that she got involved in the restaurant."

"The nice thing is that with Kate being so capable, we should be able to leave her in charge sometimes," Josh said. "When this trouble is all over, and we know our friends are safe, we might be able to go on vacation or go on some more romantic dates. All the stuff that newlyweds are supposed to do that doesn't involve running a restaurant."

"That would be nice," said Amy. "I'm looking forward to the

newlywed stuff myself. You know, after Jamie and I actually have our wedding.”

“Maybe you can all do something romantic on Valentine’s Day,” Heather suggested.

“I think on actual Valentine’s Day we’ll be busy at the restaurant, but we can have our own celebration right before or right after,” said Josh. “And I’ll get you something really nice as a present, Josie. What would you like?”

“I don’t know,” Josie said.

“Come on,” said Josh. “What do you really want?”

Josie paused and then blurted out, "I want to adopt a son."

Josh immediately started laughing. "That's a good one! That's probably the most expensive thing to ask for – taking care of a kid forever. But don't worry. I'll figure something nice out."

Heather was trying to figure out how to smooth this situation over. Though she had told Josie that there was no perfect time to bring up the adoption topic, she was certain that this was not the best way to do it. Josh had thought she was joking, and now Josie was hiding how upset she was.

However, before Heather had much of a chance to say anything, her cell phone began to ring.

"That's probably about the case," Josh said. "We should go and let you take that call."

"Good luck, Heather," Josie said.

"Thanks," Heather said before answering the call. She wasn't sure if it had to do with the case or just a developing story. It wasn't Ryan or Detective Peters that was calling. It was Hope.

Chapter 11 – Hope's Help

"I figured you out," Hope said as soon as Heather and Amy had entered the newspaper office.

"What?" asked Heather.

She and Amy had hurried over to talk to Hope in person after the phone call. She had said that she had important information that she needed to share with them, but this was not the greeting that Heather was expecting to receive.

Hope wagged a finger at them but grinned. "I know what you were really up to."

"That makes one of us," Amy muttered.

Hope explained as she showed them to the private room that they could use again. "You never really thought of me as a suspect. But you knew that this would intrigue me."

"I don't think we really thought of you as a suspect," Heather admitted. "We know you too well now. But the newspaper clippings made us need to confirm it."

"Those newspaper clippings," Hope said. "But you really should have just come out and asked me."

"You should just come out and tell us what you mean now," Amy retorted.

"Fine. I'll play," said Hope. "You knew that if I thought that you thought of me as a suspect, I'd want to know why. And I'd want to look into the newspaper clippings because you and the police thought that they came from the *Key West, Key News.* But you were afraid that because I can't print the story right away that I wouldn't be willing to help with the research. Don't make that mistake again. Of course I'll help when you need it! In exchange for an exclusive later."

"Of course," said Amy.

"I can see why you were hesitant to ask outright," Hope said. "It did end up being a lot of work."

Heather finally realized what was going on. While it hadn't been her plan to trick Hope into doing extra research, that must have been what happened, and it seemed like Hope had made a discovery.

"Did you confirm that what was on the Valentine I received really did come from your newspaper?" asked Heather.

"After Miguel showed me, I was able to officially confirm that it came from the *Key West, Key News.* But that's not all," Hope said excitedly. "I was also able to determine which issues it came from."

"You found out what papers it came from?" asked Heather. "For all of the threat?"

"It wasn't easy," Hope admitted. "But I did it. You see the words Heather and Shepherd were complete. I needed to find articles where your full name was used. The threat was made up of a combination of individual letters and words to spell out I'm going to kill you. That was trickier. But based on spacing, I was able to find the articles that were used. They were all about you."

"I guess that makes sense," said Heather. "If they're going to threaten someone, you might use the articles that are about that person as part of your message."

"It shows the writer put real effort into his work," said Amy.

"But did you say issues?" asked Heather. "It wasn't just one article that the sender took the letters from to make their message? If so, that could have been a good clue. Most likely, the sender would be using letters from the article about the case he cared about."

"It is multiple issues, but there's still a clue there," said Hope.

"What?" asked Amy. "That he hates Heather? We already picked up on that."

"Something that can help with the timeframe," said Hope. "The pieces that were used to make this threat all came from somewhat recent issues of our paper. All within the last month."

"That does help," Heather said. "A lot. We were looking for a way to narrow down our previous cases to find the person with the grudge and this timeframe might just help."

"So, it has to have been one of our recent cases?" asked Amy.

Heather nodded. "Either it happened just over a month ago, and the sender started reading the articles and becoming angrier, or it was a very recent case, and the sender found older copies of the paper. It's still possible to get a copy of the paper if it's a week or two old. It's much harder to get a copy from further back."

"That's right," said Hope.

"Thank you," Heather told the reporter.

"I'm glad I could help," said Hope. "I just feel bad if my writing these articles somehow contributed to the threats on your life and a murder."

"It's not your fault," said Heather. "You were just reporting the news. No one can fault you for that."

"But maybe you can see why we like to stay out of the limelight now," Amy muttered.

"Well, I'll show you the articles that the pieces came from and you can see if that's helpful," Hope said, pulling out past issues of the papers that she had marked. "But hey. Next time you want me to do some research for you, just ask. You don't need to accuse me of murder."

Chapter 12 – The Loser's Grudge

"Are you sure about this?" Amy asked.

"It seems like a good place to start to me," said Heather.

"I meant visiting this potential killer without Ryan and Peters," said Amy. "If this guy is really out to get you, I think we should have back up."

"I told them where we were," said Heather. "And I really want to get this investigation underway. I hate looking over my shoulder all the time. I want to find some answers soon."

"I understand," said Amy. "But what if this answer wants to kill us."

"I'm confident we can take care of ourselves," Heather said.

Then she walked up to the door of the suspect. She and Amy were visiting Sheldon Smith at home. They had met the man when he was a mayoral candidate when one of his volunteers had been murdered. He had been a suspect for a while, but in the end, thanks to Heather and Amy, he was cleared, and the rightful killer had been caught. However, Sheldon Smith did lose the special election to become mayor.

Maybe he had warped the scenario in his mind to blame Heather for his defeat.

This was a recent case, and Heather thought it was worth looking into. The winner of the mayoral race was just beginning her reign and would soon be instituting some changes in town. Maybe this had caused Sheldon Smith to snap.

Heather knocked on the door. A few moments later it opened, and a surprised Sheldon Smith greeted them.

"Hello," he said. "I didn't expect to see you two again. This isn't about that murder case again, is it? I would be more than willing to testify in court, but I thought that the killer confessed to the crime.”

“No. We’re not here because of what happened to your volunteer,” said Heather. “We’re actually investigating a new case.”

Sheldon Smith frowned. “I don’t see how I could be involved. I haven’t gone out much lately. I’ve been licking my wounds after my defeat and taking some time to myself.”

“You might have some information anyway,” said Heather. “Do you mind if we ask you some questions?”

"Sure. Would you like to come inside?" he asked, opening the door wider.

"I don't know," Amy said nervously. "Do we want to come inside? What if we're not able to come back out?"

"We'd love to come inside," Heather said decisively. "It's better to have a conversation like this in private."

He showed them into his living room and then gestured to some cookies on the table.

"My wife made some snickerdoodles if you would like

some," he said. "It's part of her campaign to cheer me up. Lots of cookies. I'm afraid she's not in at the moment though."

"They look delicious," Heather said.

Amy looked at them nervously, but Heather decided to accept a snack and put Sheldon Smith at ease. He couldn't have been expecting them to show up at his door and he wouldn't have had time to add any poison to the cookies. The only thing dangerous could be if they were disgusting and she'd need to feign a compliment. However, they ended up being quite tasty, and Heather said so.

"My wife will be glad to hear that – especially coming from a professional baker like you," Sheldon said. "But what is it that you want to discuss? Is it about my opponent? I'm afraid I haven't been keeping up with the news since I lost. I won't even let the local paper come inside. Did my opponent do something wrong? Can I give evidence against her somehow?"

"That's not exactly what we're here for," said Heather.

"What is it then?" asked Sheldon.

"Could you tell us where you were yesterday morning?" asked Heather.

Sheldon frowned. "Mitcham didn't do anything to get impeached. You think that I did something to her. But no, I couldn't have. That morning I was at the mechanic. The check engine light came on the night before, and I brought it in. I was there a very long time."

"And where was your wife that morning?" asked Amy.

"I didn't make her come with me," Sheldon said. "She usually calls her sisters around that time. It's a weekly thing when her nieces are at some activity. They catch up.

She enjoys it. So I went to the mechanic alone.”

Heather nodded. So far, it seemed like he had an alibi for the time of the murder. If he really wasn't getting the local paper, that also seemed to dismiss him as a suspect. However, Heather wanted to ask one more question to be certain.

“Did you hear about the murder that occurred behind my donut shop?”

“No. I didn't,” Sheldon said, sounding shocked.

“We think the killer was really after Heather,” said Amy.

"That's awful," Sheldon said.
"And it is really a shame that I
didn't win the election! I might
have been able to do more to
clean up this town. And keep nice
citizens like you safe."

Chapter 13 – Strawberries and Suspects

After talking to Sheldon Smith, Heather and Amy returned to Donut Delights to figure out who they wanted to talk to next. Business was steady, but it wasn't anything that her assistants couldn't handle.

Heather and Amy sat down at a table and took out the tablet of case notes again.

"What do you think about Sheldon Smith?" Amy asked.

"I'm not sure. Before we spoke to him, I thought he seemed like a prime suspect," said Heather. "But now I don't know."

"Agreed. At first, I could see the disgraced politician wanting to take revenge on someone," said Amy. "But now I think he has been home eating snickerdoodles and not plotting crimes."

"The timeframe would have fit, but he did seem genuinely surprised when I told him about the murder happening by my shop."

"I'll have Jamie help us confirm Sheldon Smith's alibi," Amy offered. "Jamie's always itching to help with our cases. And he'd be really proud to help with this one when someone is after you. Jamie uses the same mechanic

for his mobile grooming van that
Sheldon Smith mentioned before
we left. I think Jamie could get
the mechanic to talk."

"That's a great plan," Heather
said. "We'd have to see if we
could get the phone records for
the Smith home to determine if
his wife's alibi checks out too."

"You think she might be the
killer?" asked Amy.

Heather shrugged. "I bet she's
upset that Sheldon lost and is
taking it so hard. She might have
wanted vengeance just as much
as he did. And she wasn't a part
of the first case. Maybe she didn't

know how much we did to clear
his name and find the real killer."

"While the alibis are being
checked out, what should we do
next?" asked Amy. "Besides take
a Chocolate Covered
Strawberries Donut from your
display case?"

"Go ahead."

Amy didn't waste a second. She
went up to the counter and
commandeered a few donuts for
herself and Heather. Then she
returned to the table. Heather
used that time to organize her
thoughts and look at the notes on
the tablet. After talking to Hope, it
seemed like the threat writer and

killer must have started their deadly fixation on Heather recently. One of their recent cases was most likely the cause.

"Who should we interview next?" Amy asked before gobbling up a donut.

"I've been trying to think of recent cases where someone might not have liked the outcome," said Heather. "And I've come up with two that popped into my head."

"Which ones?"

"Well, the last case we investigated has some potential. I don't think the original host of Valen-Tiny Dates liked who we caught as the killer," said Heather. "And then there's Taylor Sparks."

"The bartender at the karaoke bar with the nice voice?" asked Amy.

Heather nodded. "Her father was arrested when we solved that crime."

"They do seem like two good suspects," said Amy. "Maybe one of them did decide to take their anger out on you. And Wendy from Valen-Tiny Dates might have wanted to send you the threat on a Valentine's heart because of her event."

"So, we should talk to her first," Heather agreed.

"I think there's someone else we're going to have to talk to before that," said Amy, pointing. Josie was walking toward Donut Delights and hurried over to them once she was inside.

"Have you made any progress with your case?" Josie asked.

"We think we have a strong lead to follow now," said Heather. "We have a timeframe for the newspapers used, and that seems likely that the grudge would have begun around this time."

"That's good," Josie said, sitting with them.

"And I know that you care about my safety very much," said Heather. "But did you really come here to talk about Josh and the adoption?"

"It was for both reasons," Josie admitted. She sighed. "I don't know what to do. Josh thought I was joking. He laughed at the idea of adopting."

"He didn't know all the details that you were thinking of," said Heather.

"And in that context, it did sound a little funny," said Amy. "Like me asking for a pony."

"It's not just that he didn't realize I was serious," said Josie. "He's also talking about vacations and enjoying time as newlyweds too. I want that too, but I also want to give Nicolas a home. I feel like we were a part of that hostage situation that time for a reason. I think it happened because I was meant to become his mother."

"Why don't you just tell Josh that?" asked Heather.

"What if he laughs at that too?" Josie said sadly.

"Josie," Amy said firmly. "He's your husband. You've got to talk to him. I know I'm a bit of blabbermouth, so it comes easier to me. But you've got to bet I'm going to tell Jamie everything that's on my mind. And this is clearly on your mind."

"I can usually talk to Josh about anything," Josie said. "But this just feels so…important. This is our first big decision as a married couple that we might not be on the same page for. Moving to Key West was an easy decision. Finding our house was fun. It was simple to decide to support the restaurant because it was Josh's dream and I knew it would make us both happy. And we do both want to have kids. But right now, I want Nicolas to be our son. And I'm not sure he'll feel the same."

"I think you should tell him that you weren't joking before, but that you know it's a decision that requires thought. Tell him to think about it before he gives you an answer."

Josie nodded. "I'm sorry to bother you with my problems when you have a much bigger one going on."

"I love you and Josh and Nicolas," said Heather. "It's not a bother."

"But we do have some suspects that we need to track down now," said Amy. "So, you go talk to Josh, and we'll go talk to some potential murderers."

Josie laughed. "In this situation, I'm not sure which is scarier."

Chapter 14 – Valen-Teeny Dates

Heather and Amy had finally tracked down the suspect that they wanted to speak to. However, the location for the interview was not what they were expecting.

They had met Wendy during their last investigation. She was supposed to be the host for a speed dating event called Valen-Tiny Dates where singles had quick five-minute dates with multiple people in one night to see if they had any chemistry. Wendy had been sick for the night, and someone else had filled in as the host, but Heather and Amy still had to question her.

The night had not gone as
planned. Heather and Amy had
brought donuts (and their friend
who was having some romantic
troubles) to the event, but it was
there that they had also
discovered that a single male had
been murdered. The investigators
eventually solved who had killed
the man with a blow to the head
in the men's room, and it had
been one of Wendy's friends.
She was most likely not pleased
by the results of the investigation
and might hold a grudge against
Heather.

They were hoping to talk to
Wendy at home, but it appeared
she was hosting an afternoon

speed dating event. They headed into the restaurant where they saw the signs for "Valen-Teeny Dates."

"Do you think they needed to rebrand after a murder happened at the last event?" asked Amy. "Or was this planned as a separate event to begin with?"

"I'm not sure."

"We haven't started quite yet," a voice called. "You're a little early."

They saw Wendy walking up to them, but then paused as she recognized them. She held her clipboard close to her chest.

"You're not part of this event.
What are you doing here?"

"We wanted to ask you a few
questions," said Heather.

"Really?" asked Wendy. "Just a
few questions. You're not here to
find another dead body that ruins
the reputation of my speed dating
events so much that I need to
change the name?"

"Well, that explains that," said
Amy.

"Or are you here to get another
one of my friends arrested?"
asked Wendy angrily.

"I know that you don't like what happened," said Heather. "But we didn't cause any of these events. We just explained what happened after we found all the clues. We didn't cause the murder to happen or choose that the guilty person would be someone you care about."

"Yeah. You can't shoot the messenger," said Amy. "Or the delivery person."

"Whatever," Wendy said. "What do you really want? What do you have questions about?"

"It's a new case," Heather explained. "And we think the

162

person responsible is someone linked to a recent case of ours.”

“So I’m a suspect?” asked Wendy.

“We’d just like to have a few minutes to ask you some questions about where you were at the time of the crime and if you have a motive,” Heather said calmly.

“Fine,” Wendy said, taking out a remote control. “This can be just like one of my speed dates. You can have five minutes to ask me the questions you like. Then I need to finish setting up for my event.”

She clicked a button on the remote, and the large countdown clock in the center of the room began counting down from five minutes.

"Is this really necessary?" asked Heather.

"Yes," said Wendy. "I don't want to talk to you any more than I have to. And you're wasting your question time."

"That's overly dramatic," Amy scoffed.

"This is a serious matter," said Heather. "We're investigating a murder."

"One minute down," said Wendy. "And I still don't see what I have to do with any murder cases. The only people I'm really angry at right now are you both."

"Well, that takes care of motive," said Amy. "The killer was trying to shoot Heather, but mistook someone else for her."

"What?" asked Wendy, looking less obstinate and more concerned. "Someone tried to kill you?"

"That's right," said Heather. "I received a Valentine note saying that someone intended to kill me. Then another redheaded young woman was killed outside of my donut shop."

"That's awful," said Wendy. "I don't really want you dead. I just want you to feel bad about how what happened affected my life."

"Of course we feel bad that your business was affected and someone you trusted was a killer," said Heather.

"But I don't want anyone coming after Heather because of it," said Amy.

"Well, it wasn't me," said Wendy.

"Where were you yesterday morning?" asked Heather.

"Probably home asleep," said Wendy. "I've been throwing more Valen-Teeny Date events to try and get some good press. If people find love before Valentine's Day, they'll be happy. People won't be focused on the murder. This one is in the afternoon, but most of them are at night. They can go really late, and I like to sleep in the next day. I'm trying to take care of myself after how sick I was last week."

"Can anyone corroborate this?" asked Heather.

"I'm sure lots of people can tell you I was at the Valen-Teeny Date event the night before. But I don't think anyone can tell you I was at home. I was there alone, and I turned the sound off on my phone," Wendy explained.

The buzzer sounded, signaling that five minutes had passed.

"Time's up," said Wendy.

"Well, thank you for that time," said Heather.

"I need to get ready for this to start," said Wendy as she began to walk away. "But for what it's worth, I hope you do catch the person responsible."

Chapter 15 – The Singing Suspect

After speaking to Wendy, Heather and Amy made their way to the karaoke bar where the next suspect worked. They had first met her at the same bar when they were questioning her about her ex-boyfriend's death.

That time that they visited had also been in the afternoon, and the bar had been nearly empty. Now there were quite a few people inside the place. They were all watching Taylor Sparks perform on the karaoke stage.

Heather and Amy found a place to stand and watch the show. Amy muttered about how they should take time to eat at one of the restaurants that they visited during their questions. However, when Taylor started her next song, she and the rest of the room fell silent. Taylor sang a mournful ballad that was beautiful and brought tears to the eyes of most people in the audience.

Heather and Amy applauded with the rest when she was finished.

"That was certainly a sad song," said Amy. "Maybe she's still in mourning over what happened."

"Then, the question is whether she decided to deal with her angst by targeting me," said Heather.

After the audience begged for an encore, Taylor sang one more song that was a little more upbeat. When she finished, she bowed several times as the applause continued.

"Thank you all," Taylor said, speaking into the microphone after her bows. "You've all been wonderful audience members, customers, and karaoke performers yourselves. I know I keep getting requests to come up here and sing because it's my last day, but I really can't hog it all the time. The point of a place like this is that everyone has a turn. So, the next person, get up here! I promise I'll sing another song before I go."

She headed to the edge of the stage and handed the microphone off to another potential singer. Then she left the stage.

"Where is she going to go?" asked Amy.

"I don't know. But I think we should find out," said Heather.

She led the way, and they hurried over to intercept Taylor. They weren't sure what sort of reaction they would get from her, but Taylor smiled as they approached.

"Hello there," she said. "Did you come to wish me good luck too?"

"I'm afraid we're out of the loop," said Heather. "What are you up to now?"

"I'm headed to California," Taylor said proudly. "I have a singing part in a film."

"That's amazing," said Amy.

"I think so too," Taylor said. "It's a small part right now, but it will let people hear my voice. And I think it's a great opportunity. I'm finally about to live my dream and be a professional singer."

"That's wonderful news," said Heather. "When did you find out about that?"

"Just a few days ago," Taylor said. "I'm working my final shifts so I can see everyone before I go. And then I'm boarding a flight to sunny Los Angeles."

"Yeah. Because Key West isn't sunny," Amy joked.

"If you didn't know about this, why are you here?" Taylor asked, eyeing them suspiciously. "Did you want to do some more karaoke? Last time you didn't seem like you were that into it."

"It was more like we were forced to sing in order to get you to talk to us," Amy corrected her.

"We're actually here investigating another case," said Heather.

"Really?" asked Taylor. "I don't think anything happened around the bar. And if this is about the man my dad worked for, I don't know much about him. I don't know if he's involved in anything criminal. I can't help."

"It's more that we know that our current case is related to a case we worked on recently," said Amy. "So, we're looking into recent cases. Seeing how those involved are doing. And it does seem like you are doing well. Much better than I would have expected.”

“It’s funny how the world works, isn’t it?” asked Taylor. “I’ve been trying to become a professional singer basically my whole life. My boyfriend gets murdered soon after we break up. Of course, I’m mad and devastated at the same time. Then, my dad gets taken away. I just sort of stopped caring about the consequences. I auditioned for things I never thought I’d get in a million years. But then I got one! I’m going to be in a movie!”

"But you are upset about what happened to your dad?" asked Heather.

"I'm upset about what he did," said Taylor. "I know he was trying to help, but he went about it the wrong way. I'm kind of angry with him. But he is my dad. I'll still come and visit him in jail. But I'm going to focus on my own life now. Not my dad's. Not a romantic partner's. Mine."

"Still," Amy said. "You mentioned not caring about the consequences. Someone who doesn't care about consequences might be willing to break the law to follow through with a grudge."

"What grudge?" asked Taylor. "I'm feeling good about the direction my life is taking now. I'm not holding any grudges. I don't like that such a tragedy had to occur in order for me to get what I want. But I'm happy with what is happening now."

"And you don't bear any ill will toward Heather?" asked Amy.

"No," Taylor said, looking confused. "Why would I? She caught the person who killed my boyfriend. And because of all this, I'm now on my way to becoming a movie star."

"Just one more question," said Heather. "Where were you yesterday morning?"

"I must have been running around doing errands. As soon as I found out about my movie, I've been trying to get things in place for my move before work. I'm sorry I can't be more specific. It's all a bit of a blur."

"We wish you all the best in California," Heather said.

Taylor thanked them for the good wishes and then headed back to the stage where she was being called for an encore.

Chapter 16 – Special Delivery

The next day, Heather went into Donut Delights early. She was hiding in the kitchen again, baking in a frenzy to fill the orders before Valentine's Day. Nina and Janae were helping her with the recipes and keeping her mind off her troubles. She just didn't feel like she was close to solving this case. She had been stuck on cases before, but never when her life could be in immediate danger. Why couldn't she make sense of the clues now?

"I got another clue," Nina said.

"Really?" asked Heather, looking worried. "Another threat arrived?"

"No," Nina said quickly. "And I didn't mean to scare you."

"I'm sorry," Heather said. "My mind keeps circulating back to the case. I should have realized what you meant. You got another Valentine message from Nick?"

Nina nodded. "This one said: It takes two of us. I'm glad it's you and me."

"That is sweet," said Heather.

"Do you have any idea what it could be?" Nina asked.

"I do have a guess," Heather admitted. "But I promised Nick

that I wouldn't interfere. He wants you to figure it out."

"I'm just not sure what it is," said Nina. "It seems like there are too many possibilities."

"I'm having the same problem," said Heather. "But that's unfortunate because it means that there are lots of potential people who could want to kill me. That's not a happy thought."

"I don't understand it," said Janae, piping up. "People should be happy when you solve a case. Not blame you. I was really grateful when you solved that crime on the bike trail when we first met."

"I just wish we could help you figure this out," Nina said. "Who is after you?"

"Agreed," said Janae. "I don't like thinking someone is out to kill my boss and friend. And I would be happy to take this silly Valentine hat off my head."

Heather listened as she heard someone enter the shop and greet Luz.

"I think that's Amy," Heather said. "Maybe between all four of us, we can talk out the case and get an answer."

"Whatever you need, boss," Janae said.

Amy entered the kitchen. After she said hello, she had some news to report. "Jamie was able to talk to the mechanic. Sheldon Smith really was there at the time of the murder."

"So, he's definitely eliminated as a suspect," Heather said.

"I know I wanted Mitcham to win the race, but I didn't think of Smith as a killer," said Janae.

"But he was really disappointed that he lost and he might have blamed Heather for the case somehow," said Amy. "And that's why his wife is still a suspect. Maybe she tried to kill Heather on his behalf."

"Does she have an alibi?" asked Nina.

"Ryan checked, and there was a long phone call placed from the Smith household that morning," said Heather. "But it's possible to fake an alibi like that. She might have called her sister and told her not to hang up the phone for an hour so it would look like they had been talking all that time."

"Devious," said Amy.

"Who else do you have as a suspect?" asked Janae.

"It's possible that it could be anyone who was involved in a case Heather worked on and didn't like the result," said Amy. "But it was most likely one of our recent cases because all of the newspaper clippings on the Valentine came from articles about her this past month."

"We spoke to Taylor Sparks, whose father was arrested, but it doesn't seem like she is holding a grudge," said Heather. "It is possible that she was threatening me because she was about to leave town, but she just seemed very happy when we saw her."

"Wendy didn't seem happy," said Amy. "She seemed angry with us. And she had a weak alibi. She said she was home alone asleep."

"So, do you think she did it?" asked Nina.

Heather was about to say that she was unsure, but then she heard movement by the back door of Donut Delights. She took a few steps toward it.

"Oh no," Nina said nervously. "Is someone there? Is it the killer?"

Heather opened the door quickly, hoping that if it was someone dangerous, they could catch him by surprise. She was successful in surprising the man but didn't sense any danger from him.

A deliveryman from the produce store dropped his clipboard in surprise.

"Sorry," he said. "I guess I'm a little jumpy because of what happened to Bonnie. But you must be someone who works at Donut Delights."

"I'm the owner," she responded.

"We were told that the police would allow us to make deliveries again, so I brought your produce order," he explained. "I volunteered to do it because I thought I was the bravest one for this route. I guess that wasn't quite the case."

"I can understand your being nervous," Heather said. "Why don't you bring the produce in right away and then we'll give you one of our donuts as thanks."

"A thank you to you too," he said happily.

Heather went back inside to explain to the others who was there and prepare some donut choices for him. The delivery man quickly brought the produce inside and to the proper place. Then Heather asked which donut he would like. He chose the

Chocolate Covered Strawberries Donut, and she told him it was a wise selection.

They made some small talk about future deliveries, but then something started to bother Heather. She stared at him for a moment.

"Your uniform says the name of the produce company on the front of your shirt," Heather said.

"That's right," the man said. "They want everyone to know that the fresh fruit we're delivering is from them."

Something finally clicked into
place in Heather's head, and she
nearly gasped.

"What is it?" Amy asked when
she saw the look on her friend's
face.

"I've been looking at this all
wrong," Heather said.
"Completely wrong."

"What do you mean?" asked
Nina.

"Bonnie Purvis was shot in the
chest," Heather said.

"Right," Amy said as the delivery
man shuddered.

"You can take those hats off now," Heather told her assistants. "I finally figured out how this all fits together."

"You know who is after you?" asked Janae, taking the opportunity to take off her hat.

"I know who the killer is," said Heather.

Chapter 17 – Catching a Killer

Heather tried to remain calm as she stood near the counter at Donut Delights after hours. She thought about eating one of her delicious donuts, but it would be hard to enjoy one when she knew that she was the bait to catch a killer.

She had laid traps for killers before, but it was scary to know that this killer definitely had a gun and that his sole purpose for coming here was to dispose of her.

She hoped she was far back enough from the windows that she couldn't get hurt. She needed the killer to come inside and show his hand. She pretended to keep busy until she heard someone at the door.

"Come on in," she said, not leaving the counter. "It's open. I'm expecting someone to pick up a late night order. Come inside."

Bill Purvis followed her directions and entered the shop. His eyes were darting around the place, trying to figure out if they were alone. Heather walked behind the counter to put some distance between them under the guise of getting some donuts.

"I'm glad you came," Heather said. "It must be difficult for you to be alone. I'm sorry you lost your wife just before Valentine's Day. Let me get you some donuts so you'll have something sweet to eat."

"Why don't you come out from behind that counter?" he suggested. "I want to talk to you about the case. And what happened to Bonnie."

"I'm afraid I'm not going to come any closer," Heather said. "I don't want you to shoot me."

"What?" Bill Purvis asked. He laughed as if it were ridiculous. "Why would I shoot you?"

"I think the better question is why would you shoot your wife?"

"What?" Bill asked again. This time he wasn't laughing.

"It was a pretty clever plan. You wanted us to think that the killer was after me all this time, but you actually did kill the person you wanted to: your wife."

"What are you saying?"

"I'm saying I figured it out," Heather explained. "Your wife got transferred to her new delivery route about a month ago. You realized that she bore a resemblance to me, at least in body type and hair color, and you developed a plan. It became clear when you realized how much my name was mentioned in the local news. You collected news stories on me and sent me a threat. I kept wondering why a killer would announce that he was out to get me. But then I realized that was the point. You needed us to think that the killer was after me and not after Bonnie."

Bill just shook his head.

"But the killer had to have known that it wasn't me that they shot. Bonnie was shot in the chest. Not in the back. Besides the differences in our faces, Bonnie's uniform proclaimed that she was a delivery driver. Someone who had been plotting to kill me for so long should have seen the difference," said Heather. "And once I realized that Bonnie Purvis was the intended victim, everything began to make a lot more sense. I realized it must have been you who killed her because of how you acted at the police station. You made such a point to say that I looked like your wife. And you were careful not to admit that you knew we thought that I was the intended victim then. It was all very clever."

"Thank you," Bill said finally. An evil smile had formed on his face.

"And now you've come here to shoot me because you're afraid

that we might suspect that no one is really after me."

"They should think that someone is after you," Bill said. "You're sticking your nose into cases all the time. When I read about you in the paper, I knew I couldn't have picked a better red herring."

"But why did you want to kill Bonnie?"

"Oh. The usual reasons why a husband wants his wife out of the way," Bill said, advancing toward her. "The insurance money. The chance to find someone younger."

"That's awful."

"But you. You get to die because you know too much. I might have only needed to fire some shots at you to get them to think that the killer was still out there. It's a very common gun, and they wouldn't be able to trace it to me. Bonnie thought it was stolen a year ago," Bill said, taking out the gun. "But now I'm going to have to take you out. And I'll enjoy it."

"Not so fast!"

Heather turned pale as she saw Nick and Mr. Rankle barge into the shop. Nick was holding some of the novelty baseball bats that their store sold and Mr. Rankle

was holding bug spray like it was
a weapon.

"What's this?" Bill asked.

"No one messes with my
neighbors," Mr. Rankle said
before spraying the bug repellant
straight into the attacker's eyes.

Bill was so surprised he didn't
react in time to block the spray.
He dropped the gun as he cried
out in pain.

Nick was about to knock the man
down with the baseball bats, but
then Ryan and Peters ran out
from the back room.

"What's going on?" Mr. Rankle asked.

"We overheard everything," Ryan explained. "We were about to make our presence known when we heard you enter. We wanted to make sure that you weren't his backup in case we needed to sneak around first."

"You mean I didn't need to barge in here and try to protect my neighbor?" Mr. Rankle asked.

"No," said Heather. "But it was very much appreciated. You both were willing to face an armed killer to save my life."

"Bah," Mr. Rankle replied.

Ryan and Peters read Bill Purvis his rights and escorted him out of the donut shop. Amy came out from the back room as well.

"You don't know how hard it was for me not to make a comment when he called you a red herring," Amy said.

"There's definitely a case against Bill Purvis for murder now," Heather said. "And it's nice for me to know that I have neighbors who are willing to be heroes."

She beamed at them.

"You would have done the same for us," Nick said.

"The bug spray I wasted cost six dollars," said Mr. Rankle. "And I expect you to pay me back for it."

Chapter 18 – Valentine's Day

"Thanks," Amy said as Heather handed her some donuts. "This is the perfect thing to bring on our romantic picnic."

"It's going to be the best Valentine's Day ever," Jamie agreed. "Because I get to spend it with my fiancée. But who knows? Maybe it will be even better in the future if I get to spend it with my wife."

"I'll look forward to testing that," said Amy.

Heather smiled at her friends. They were all at Donut Delights. It felt good to be there when it was not part of a crime scene or as a part of a trap to lure in a murderer. They would be closing early for Valentine's Day so that her assistants could still enjoy romantic evenings off, and customers were hurrying to get their orders before they closed.

"Well, enjoy your picnic," Heather said.

Amy and Jamie promised that they would and then left the shop. Janae walked up to Heather then.

"It's official."

"What?" asked Heather.

"The Chocolate Bike Tour," Janae said happily. "Fire Frank

and I found the perfect trail, so next year it's on the schedule leading up to Valentine's Day. I know people will love to try your chocolate donuts and a lot will be bought. I hope this gives you enough time to get ready."

"I think it will," Heather said with a wink.

"Ready for what?" Nina asked, joining them.

"A chocolate bike tour," said Heather. "But what about you? Are you ready for your date tonight? Did you figure out what it is?"

"I think so," Nina said. "I think we're going to go dancing. I should wear shoes that I could move in. And I think in the latest card he was referring to the phrase: it takes two to tango. What do you think of my guess?"

"It's the same one I had," said Heather. "You're on your way to becoming a sleuth yourself!"

Nina laughed. "That's too dangerous for me. I'll stick to baking."

Heather smiled at her assistants. However, her smile grew even more when she saw Ryan stroll inside the shop with some red roses.

"I thought you might not want a card after everything that happened," he explained. "But I thought you could never go wrong with roses."

"You can say that again," Heather said, accepting the bouquet. "Thank you."

"How are you feeling?" he asked.

"Surprised to see you so early," she responded. "But very happy."

"I meant about the case. But I am glad that you're still happy when I visit you at work."

"It's only fair. You're happy when I visit you at the station too," said Heather. "And I'm really glad this case is over. I feel like a great weight has been lifted off my shoulders now that I know no one is after me and that it's not my fault the poor woman was killed."

"It was never your fault," Ryan said. "But it is because of you that her killer was brought to justice. And I thought because of the case being solved and because of Valentine's Day, we should do something to celebrate."

"I love the idea. What did you have in mind?"

"I think it might be too late to get a reservation somewhere, but I bet Josh and Josie would give us some delicious takeout from J+J's. We can have some of your donuts, and I'll pick up a bottle of champagne," said Ryan. "Eva is going out with her beau, Vincent, but Leila said she would love to babysit Lilly. We can have some time to ourselves, not worrying about a case. And then maybe watch a movie with them tonight."

"That sounds absolutely perfect," Heather said and then she kissed him.

The End.

A letter from the Author

To each and every one of my Amazing readers: I hope you enjoyed this story as much as I enjoyed writing it. Let me know what you think by leaving a review!

Stay Curious,
Susan Gillard